The Christmas Thingy

By F. Paul Wilson

Pictures by Alan M. Clark

Cemetery Dance Publications
Baltimore
2000

Text copyright © 2000 by F. Paul Wilson

Illustration copyright © 2000 by Alan M. Clark

Book design by Alan M. Clark

Published by Cemetery Dance Publications

ISBN 1-58767-031-3

Cemetery Dance Publications
P.O. Box 943
Abingdon MD 21009
U.S.A.

http://www.cemeterydance.com

Printed in Canada

First Edition

10 9 8 7 6 5 4 3 2 1

Dedicated to Ethan Paul Bateman and Hannah Elizabeth Bowers

Alan M. Clark wishes to thank Melody Kees Clark for her assistance with Thingy's note, and Jill Bauman for sharing her design ideas for Thingy.

A NOTE TO THE READER

THE CHRISTMAS THINGY is meant to be read aloud. So if you're reading this to your children, or to your little brother or sister, try using different voices as you go along: Use your regular voice for Jessica; use a high-pitched British voice for Mrs. Murgatroyd; and hold your nose whenever the Thingy speaks.

But most of all, have fun.

"**Y**ou want *what* for Christmas?" Mrs. Murgatroyd says, bending to pick up the pieces of the plate she just dropped.

"A monster," Jessica Atkins says, nibbling on her toast. "Not a big, mean monster. I want a friendly little one to play with when I come home from school, and maybe keep me company at night."

"Don't you wish for no monster, Miss Jessica," Mrs. Murgatroyd says, her accent getting thicker with each word. "Not for Christmas! 'Specially not in *this* 'ouse!"

Jessica is sorry for upsetting the plump old housekeeper, but now she's very curious.

"What do you mean, Mrs. M.?"

"You just might get your wish!"

"Really?" Jessica claps her hands with glee. "Oh, I wish, I wish, I *wish!*"

"You'll be very sorry, you will," Mrs. Murgatroyd says in a grave tone. "Very sorry if the Christmas Thingy decides to pay you a visit."

"'Thingy?'" Jessica laughs. "'*Thingy?*' What a funny name!"

"You won't be thinkin' it's so funny when you wake up Christmas morning and find out what's 'appened to all your presents."

Suddenly Jessica is no longer smiling.

"Wh-what will happen?"

"The same thing that 'appened almost one 'undred—no, I do believe it was *exactly* one 'undred years ago."

Jessica waits patiently as the housekeeper counts the years. Mrs. Murgatroyd sort of came with the house and has worked here forever.

"Yes. It was exactly one century ago this year that the Christmas Thingy visited this very 'ouse. The lit'le boy who lived 'ere then 'ad been wishin' for a secret friend. Well, as Advent came, 'e got 'is wish: the Christmas Thingy arrived. It stayed right up until Christmas, it did, and then it left, because Thingies must always return to Thingyland before dawn on Christmas morning. But before it left this 'ouse a century ago, it stole some presents."

"Oh, that's awful!" Jessica cries.

"Not *all* the presents, mind you; not the 'ole family's. Just one person's. The ones for the lit'le boy who 'ad befriended it. The Thingy stole *all* the lit'le boy's presents and took them back to Thingyland to 'oard and gloat over, because nobody *gives* presents in Thingyland at Christmas. They *steals* them."

"But why?"

"Thingies steal," says Mrs. Murgatroyd with a shrug. "They can't 'elp it. Stealing is in their nature. As me Mum used to say, 'Like a rose must bloom and a pig must squeal, a cow must moo and a thingy must steal. It simply must.'"

"But what's a Thingy look like?"

"Ow, it's an 'ideous lit'le creature, it is. Too ugly to describe. Let's just 'ope you never 'as the misfortune o' seeing the lit'le blighter!"

Jessica nods, but inside she still wants her own little monster. Then she yawns.

"You wouldn't be tired now, would you? You just got up."

"I keep waking up and hearing noises."

"These old 'ouses is full o' creaks an' squeaks. You'll get used to 'em after you've lived 'ere a while longer."

Jessica knows that the noises come from mice in the walls—little scratchings all through the night. But she doesn't want to tell Mrs. Murgatroyd that. The housekeeper will start setting out traps. Jessica doesn't want to hurt the mice, she just wants them to go away.

She smiles as she realizes something: If she got a little monster for Christmas, maybe it would scare those mice away.

With that nice thought in her head, she tightens the thigh strap on her leg brace and gets up from the table.

"Thanks for the breakfast, Mrs. M."

The old housekeeper smiles. "You're quite welcome, Miss Jessica. But don't you be watchin' any o' those silly old movies now. You've already got enough strange notions in that lit'le eight-year-old 'ead as it is."

"What else am I going to do?" Jessica whispers as she limps up the steps to her room. "I've got nobody to play with."

Sometimes Jessica wishes her folks hadn't moved here to England. The idea of living in London for a year while her parents write an important research paper seemed so exciting last summer. But they rented this big old Victorian mansion to live in, and it's so far from where most of her classmates live that she hardly ever gets to see them.

It's not as if no one likes me, she thinks as she enters her bedroom with its high ceiling and huge bed. It's just that I can't do a lot of the things they do.

Jessica knows she's a normal little girl in every way except maybe that she likes monsters. Oh, yes...and her left leg doesn't work. People tend to forget that because Jessica tends to forget it. Her left leg has never worked since the day she was born so she's quite used to it. She has to wear a brace from her hip to her ankle to help hold her up. But she hardly ever thinks about it. She pulls on her brace every morning like other children pull on a sock.

But it means she can't ride a bike or walk very well with her braced leg, and since both her parents are doing research all day, she spends a lot of time after school alone.

Not completely alone. There's Mrs. Murgatroyd, of course, but she spends the whole day cooking and cleaning, so she's no fun.

To pass the time between the end of school and the time her mom and dad come home, Jessica watches movies on the VCR. She watches only fantasy, science fiction, and monster films. Everything from *Frankenstein* to *Godzilla* to *The Wizard of Oz* to *Star Wars* to *Gremlins*, and back again. She loves monster films the best.

But all the films in the world can't take the place of one real friend. Jessica doesn't tell her parents, but she's very lonely here in England.

And so, despite Mrs. Murgatroyd's warning, Jessica decides to keep wishing for a little

monster for Christmas. She knows it probably won't matter anyway. Wishing hardly ever works, otherwise her left leg would have been as good as her right long ago, but she also knows that Christmas is a special time in the world, and unusual things can happen in this magical season.

Very unusual things.

"**W**hat was *that?*" Jessica says, sitting up in bed and looking around in the dark. It's a chilly night in the first week of December.

"Just the wind," she tells herself. "I hope."

Despite her love of monsters and spooky movies—which she knows are only make-believe—Jessica isn't terribly fond of being alone at night in her

second floor bedroom. This room is old and dark, with high, carved ceilings and strange wallpaper. Not at all like her bedroom at home in America.

She listens carefully and hears the usual faint little scratchings of the mice as they run up and down in the spaces inside her walls. She's not afraid of mice—she's seen a couple of them and they're cute little things.

But now, she hears a different sound. A *rustling* that seems to come from under her bed. Thinking it's a mouse, she looks below with the flashlight she always keeps under her pillow (just in case there's a power failure) but sees nothing.

"Yep," she sighs. "Just the wind."

The next afternoon after school, Jessica goes to her dresser and finds that both of the candy bars she always keeps in her top drawer (in case of snack attacks) are gone. Only the empty wrappers remain.

The mice ate her candy!

At least she *thinks* it was the mice. To find out for sure, she decides to set a trap. Not a hurting trap—a tasty trap.

That night, sometime after dinner and before bedtime, while Mrs. Murgatroyd is clearing and cleaning up and Mom and Dad are having their coffee, Jessica places one of Mrs. Murgatroyd's homemade donuts on a plate on the night stand next to her bed. She ties a string to the donut, and attaches the string to a bell. Then she turns out the light and waits outside her door.

It's not long—only minutes, really—before she hears the tinkle of the bell. She leaps inside the room with her flashlight and finds...

...an empty plate.

"The donut!" Jessica cries. "Where'd the donut go?"

Then she notices a trail of crumbs leading across the carpet. She follows them to the closet and, without waiting to decide whether she should be scared or not, she pulls open the closet door and shines the light inside.

And finds two big eyes staring back at her!

Jessica lets out a little "Eek!" and turns to run, but a funny voice stops her.

"Don't be afraid, Jessica. I'm what you've been wishing for."

The voice seems friendly enough, so Jessica turns on the bedroom light and steps back.

"Come on out where I can see you," she says.

"Okay," says the voice, which sounds like someone talking while holding his nose, "but don't be scared."

And out of her closet steps the strangest little creature Jessica has ever seen. Her first thought is that it looks like an oversized mushroom with big eyes and two feet; around the edge of the mushroom cap are a bunch of twisty little tentacles. One of those tentacles is coiled around a half-eaten donut. Jessica realizes why its voice sounds like someone talking with a pinched nose—it doesn't *have* a nose!

Jessica can't help it. She begins to laugh.

"You're not afraid of me?" it says in its nasal voice.

"No! I think you're funny-looking! What on earth are you?"

"Funny? I'll have you know I'm the Christmas Thingy."

Jessica is shocked. She stops laughing.

"The one who was here a hundred years ago?"

Thingy smiles and bows. "The very same."

"The one who stole the little boy's presents?"

"Of course not! I wish I knew how that story got started. It's not true! Every time something gets lost at Christmas, I get blamed for it. It's not fair. I'm innocent!"

"I believe you!" Jessica says, feeling sorry for Thingy.

"You do? Oh, good. I've been so upset about this that it's taken me a hundred years to get up the nerve to come back. But you wished for me, so I came. And now that I'm here, I hope to restore the good name of Thingies everywhere."

"And I'll help!" Jessica says. "I'll tell Mrs. M. that—"

"Oh, no! You mustn't tell Mrs. Murgatroyd! She'll never believe me. She'll chase me back to Thingyland before I get a chance to prove myself. Let's keep it a secret from her for now. You can tell her all about me on Christmas after you've opened all your presents. That will show her."

"Does that mean we'll be secret friends?" Jessica asks.

"The very secretest. And to prove I'm your friend, I'm going to get rid of all those noisy mice scratching inside your bedroom walls at night."

"Don't hurt them!"

"I wouldn't think of it. I'm just going to send them to the basement where they won't bother you any-more."

As Jessica watches, Thingy twists its tentacles into braids and squeezes its eyes closed real tight.

"There!" it says after a moment. "They're gone."

"For good?"

"For as long as you live here."

"How do I know they're gone?"

"You'll see," says Thingy.

Later that night, as Jessica lies in her bed in the dark, she strains her ears but can't hear a single scratch in the walls. The silence is glorious!

"Thank you, Thingy," she says into the dark. "I have a feeling we're going to be great friends."

"Of course we are," says Thingy from its place under her bed.

As soon as Jessica awakens the next morning, she looks under her bed. But all she sees are a few dust bunnies.

No sign of the Christmas Thingy.

She sighs sadly. "I must have dreamed the whole thing."

But as she's pulling on her leg brace, she hears a familiar pinched-nose voice.

"What's this, Jessica?"

She looks up and there's Thingy standing by the open closet door.

"Thingy! You're here!"

"Of course I'm here. And you're there." With one of his tentacles, he holds up a black rectangular box. "But what is this contraption?"

"It's a VCR tape—a movie." She looks at the title. "That one's got no talking but it's super. It's called *The Thief of Baghdad*."

"It's about someone who steals?" Thingy asks, its eyes suddenly bright.

"Yes. And there's lots of magic stuff in it. Even a flying carpet."

"A flying carpet?" Thingy says. "That sounds like fun!"

With that, Thingy braids up its tentacles and squeezes its eyes shut, just as it did last night.

For a moment, nothing happens. Then Jessica notices a ripple running over the throw rug on the floor next to her bed. As she watches, its edges begin to flutter.

Thingy jumps on it. "Hurry, Jessica. Hop on!"

Jessica steps onto the rug and drops to her knees at its center as the rug begins to vibrate.

"What's happening!"

"We're about to have some fun!" Thingy says.

A very astonished Jessica finds herself rising into the air upon the rug.

"We're flying!" she cries.

"Yes. A flying carpet. Just like you said."

Jessica is a little scared but she's also very excited. She's flown on a plane before, but never on a carpet. She laughs as they rise almost to the ceiling, then lets out a little scream as the carpet begins to swoop about the room, diving up and down like a roller coaster.

"This is fun!" Thingy says to her. "Why didn't I ever think of it before?"

"Maybe because you never watched *The Thief of Baghdad*. If you want, we can—" Suddenly Jessica notices that they're swooping straight toward her bedside lamp. "Look out!" she cries.

"Whoops!" says Thingy as he tries to pull the carpet out of its dive. He almost makes it, but the edge of the rug catches the rim of the shade.

The lamp falls to the floor with a crash.

"Oh, no!" Jessica cries as the rug settles back to the floor. "We broke it!" Suddenly she hears footsteps on the stairs. "Hide, Thingy! Here comes Mrs. Murgatroyd!"

"Okay," says Thingy, "but first..."
Thingy braids its tentacles and scrinches up its eyes.
As an amazed Jessica watches, the broken pieces of the lamp begin to move.

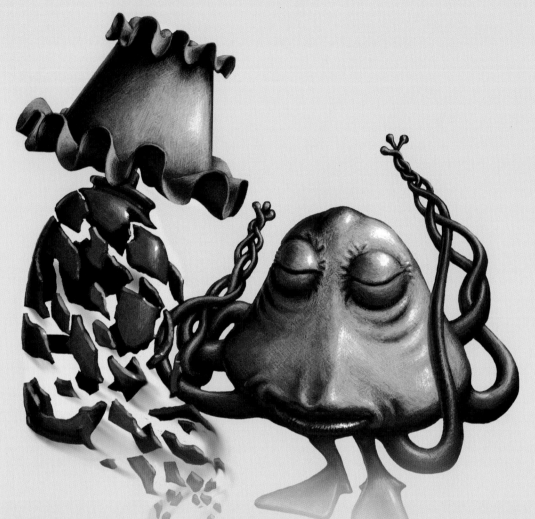

"Hurry!" Jessica whispers. "I hear her coming down the hall!"
The pieces rise into the air and begin to revolve around each other. Slowly at first, then with lightning speed, they swirl as if caught in a miniature tornado.
"She's right outside the door!" Jessica says.
Suddenly, with a flash of light, all the pieces rush together again and the lamp is as good as new.
Jessica hears the door knob turn. She looks up and sees the door beginning to open.
"Miss Jessica?" Mrs. Murgatroyd says as the door swings open.
In a single blur of motion, the lamp hops back up on the night table and Thingy dives under the bed.
"Yes, Mrs. M?" Jessica says, gulping with relief as the old housekeeper steps into

the room.

"Did you 'ear a loud noise just a moment ago?"

"Yes, I did," Jessica says. "It sounded as if a lamp had fallen and smashed on the floor."

"I dare say, that's just what it sounded like to me, as well. I thought it came from this room."

"Well, as you can see," Jessica says, pointing to her lamp, "my lamp is as good as new."

"So it is. I do believe me ears is starting to play tricks on me! Ah, well. Come downstairs now. Breakfast is ready."

"I'll be down in a minute," Jessica says.

As Mrs. Murgatroyd steps out into the hall and closes the door, Thingy sticks his head out from under the bed and winks.

Jessica laughs. This is going to be the best Christmas ever.

"I feel it in me bones," Mrs. Murgatroyd says as she sips her morning tea. "That Christmas Thingy blighter's come back."

It's been two weeks since she thought she heard Miss Jessica's lamp break, and a number of happenings have made the old housekeeper very suspicious.

First of all, there's the noises in Miss Jessica's room. Mrs. Murgatroyd has heard crashes, laughter, running feet, and, on a number of occasions, when she's listened at the door, she's heard the sound of two voices talking: Miss Jessica's, and someone else's.

Secondly, little things are missing about the house. For days now, Mr. Atkins has been looking for his favorite tie clasp; Mrs. Atkins reported yesterday that her favorite pen, the one she uses to write herself notes, is missing; and just this morning Mrs. Murgatroyd discovered that her very own tortoise shell comb is gone.

"I may not be Sherlock 'Olmes," she says to herself, "but it don't take no bloomin' genius to suspect that the Christmas Thingy is back."

Just then Jessica walks into the kitchen.

"I won't have time for breakfast this morning, Mrs. M.," she says.

"Late again?" says Mrs. Murgatroyd. "Whatever do you do in that room these past few mornings?"

"Oh...I just play."

"Well, Miss Jessica, I wouldn't be doing me duty if I didn't give you one more warning: Don't 'ave nothin' to do with that Christmas Thingy. It's bad news, it is."

"Maybe that story about the Thingy isn't true," Jessica says.

"It's true all right. And should that Thingy show up, don't you let it tell you otherwise. Thingies love to lie; they tells the truth only when necessary. And don't be forgettin': They steals. As me Mum used to say, 'Like a rose must bloom and a pig must squeal, a cow must moo and a Thingy must steal. It simply must.' You may think it's your friend, Miss Jessica, but it's obliged to return to Thingyland before dawn on Christmas morning, and when it does it will take all your presents with it."

"I have to go back upstairs for a minute," Jessica says.

Mrs. Murgatroyd nods her head slowly as she watches Jessica limp away.

"It's come back," she says to herself. "I'm sure of it now. The lit'le blighter's come back."

Jessica is worried as she hurries back up to her bedroom. She and Thingy have been having such a great time these past few weeks. Every day has been something new. Thingy is full of all sorts of magic and knows hundreds of wonderful tricks. Jessica has never had such a special friend all to herself before. She doesn't want to believe that Thingy's been lying to her.

As she bursts into her room she says, "Are you going to be my friend forever, or are you going to take all my presents and leave me on Christmas Eve?"

Thingy looks at her with its wide, innocent eyes and says, "What kind of a friend would take another friend's Christmas presents?"

"Good. I knew you wouldn't do something like that to me. See you after school."

"Bye, Jessica," says Thingy.

Later on that morning, Mrs. Murgatroyd arrives in Jessica's room with her broom. "I know you're 'ere, Mr. Thingy," she says. "An' I'm going to find you. An' when I do, I'm going to take me broom and sweep you right back to Thingyland, I am."

Mrs. Murgatroyd spends most of the morning searching Jessica's room. She searches under the bed, in the drawers, in the closet, under the night table, everywhere a Thingy might hide. In a corner under Jessica's bed she finds Mr. Atkins' tie clasp, Mrs. Atkins' pen, and her own tortoise shell comb.

But nowhere does she find a trace of the Christmas Thingy.

"I may not be too sure of many things in me life," she says to herself at last, "but I know for certain there's no Christmas Thingy in this room."

So saying, she takes her broom and leaves.

It's Christmas Eve and Jessica is wrapping the last of her presents in her bedroom.

"Who's that for?" Thingy asks.

"My mother. I made her a chain for her eyeglasses."

"I'm sure she'll love it," Thingy says. "What do you think Santa will bring you?"

"I don't know," Jessica says as she places the gift on the floor. She turns to Thingy with a big smile. "It doesn't matter. Even if he puts coal in my stocking tonight, this will still be the best Christmas ever because of you, Thingy." She takes off her leg brace and leans it in its usual spot against the night table. "We've had so much fun! And there's so much more fun to come!" She leans over and kisses Thingy on the top of its head. "Good night, my best friend."

"Good night, Jessica."

"Get to sleep now," Jessica tells Thingy as she turns off her light. "Before Santa Claus comes!"

"Okay. I will."

But Thingy doesn't go to sleep. It doesn't even crawl under the bed. Instead, it waits up in the dark until after it hears Santa Claus come and go. Then it sneaks downstairs.

Thingy doesn't want to steal Jessica's presents. It really likes Jessica, but it can't help itself. Like a rose must bloom and a pig must squeal, a cow must moo and a Thingy must steal. It simply must.

As Thingy peeks into the great living room, it sees the big Christmas tree all alight, and sees all the presents piled around it. Thingy wishes they had Christmas like this in Thingyland. It would be so much better than stealing.

Suddenly Thingy spies a dark figure in the corner by the fireplace. It's Mrs. Murgatroyd, standing guard over the presents with her broom, ready to sweep an unwary Thingy back to Thingyland.

But Thingy knows how to take care of her. It braids up its tentacles and squeezes its eyes shut, and in less than a minute Mrs. Murgatroyd is sound asleep.

Safe now, Thingy approaches the tree and starts picking out all of Jessica's presents. Then it carries them up to Jessica's bedroom. This is tough work because Santa has left Jessica so many presents. As Thingy gets ready to push the presents under the bed to take them back to Thingyland, it spies a little gift-wrapped box sitting all alone under the bed.

Thingy pulls out the box and looks at the tag. It reads, *"To Thingy from your pal, Jessica."*

Thingy can't believe it. Quickly it tears the box open and inside finds a tiny Christmas tree deco-rated with miniature balls and strung with tiny garland.

A tear forms in Thingy's eye. No one has ever given it a Christmas present be-fore—or *any* present, for that matter. It simply isn't done in Thingy-land.

Thingy is suddenly very upset. This ruins all its plans. How can it steal Jessica's presents after Jessica gave it one for its very own? The Christmas Thingy knows that Thingies must steal, but it can't take Jessica's presents now, it simply can't!

Thingy hurries back downstairs and replaces the presents under the tree, then returns to Jessica's bedroom.

Thingy knows it has to get back to Thingyland before dawn. There's not much time left, and it must steal *something* to bring back with it...it simply must. But what? It doesn't want to take anything Jessica will miss. *What…?*

Suddenly Thingy has an idea. A wonderful idea! It knows just what to steal. It braids up its tentacles, scrinches its eyes shut, and starts the magic...

Jessica awakens the next morning to find a note beside her bed:

Dear Jessica—
I had to return to Thingyland and I had to steal something, I simply had to. So I took something you won't be needing.
Your Friend,
The Christmas Thingy

With her heart pounding, a very worried Jessica slips out from under her covers and looks under the bed. Thingy is gone, and so is the present she left for it. Missing her friend already, she runs downstairs to see if Mrs. Murgatroyd has been right all along.

But no. She finds lots of presents for her under the tree. Jessica wakes Mrs. Murgatroyd, then rushes back up to her room and looks around. There's no sign of Thingy, and she can't imagine what is missing.

What could Thingy have taken?

Suddenly Jessica gasps and looks down at her left leg. She forgot to put on her brace and yet here she is standing without it.

"It works! My leg works!"

She looks over by the night stand—the brace is gone! And then she remembers Thingy's note:

I took something you won't be needing

"Mommy! Daddy!" she cries, and runs down the hall on her two good legs to show them how her friend the Christmas Thingy left her the best Christmas gift of all.

But in the back of her mind she wonders what will Thingy ever do with her old leg brace?

The End

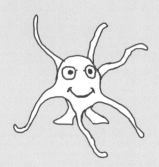

F. PAUL WILSON is the award-winning, bestselling author of more than twenty novels and dozens of short stories. Over six million copies of his books are in print in the US and his work has been translated into twenty-four foreign languages. He also has written for the stage, screen, and interactive media.

ALAN M. CLARK has been a free-lance illustrator since 1984. He is the recipient of the World Fantasy Award and four Chesley Awards.